T0197515

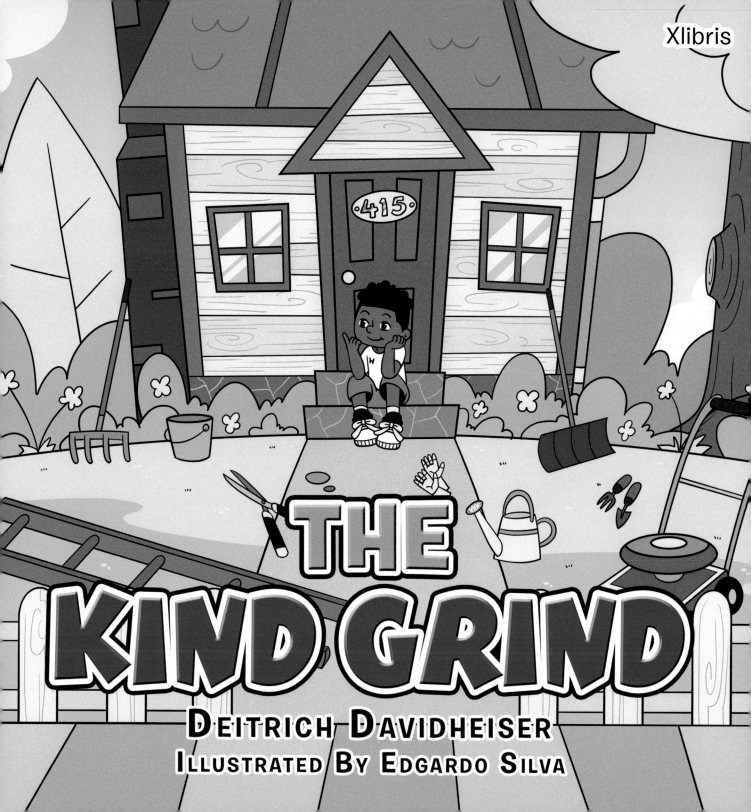

Xlibris

THE KIND GRIND

DEITRICH DAVIDHEISER

ILLUSTRATED BY EDGARDO SILVA

To order additional copies of this book, contact:
Xlibris
844-714-8691
www.Xlibris.com
Orders@Xlibris.com

ISBN: Softcover   978-1-6698-4414-3
        EBook   978-1-6698-4413-6

Print information available on the last page

Rev. date: 10/04/2022

'THE KIND GRIND' FOCUSES ON 3 KEY VALUES

Vision

The power to see future events or ideas with imagination!

Hardwork

The ability to put in extra effort even when everyone else quits!

Kindness

The act of being friendly and generous without expecting a gift in return!

1. The importance of **vision**
2. The value of **hardwork**
3. The power of **kindness**

Henry jumped out of bed, excited about a big idea in his head!

Christmas just passed and it was real tough, he and his cousins barely got any stuff.

But next year will be different, Henry has a big plan.

To start his own business, and shape up the neighborhood with his bare hands!

He pulled out his crayons and started to scribble.

On the top, the bottom, as well as the middle!

3

And when he was done, he jumped to his feet!

And saw right away, work was not yet complete!

In order for Henry's complete satisfaction, he hurried to put his plan into action!

Henry looked outside and saw the sun going down.

So, he jumped on his bike to hang his flyers around town!

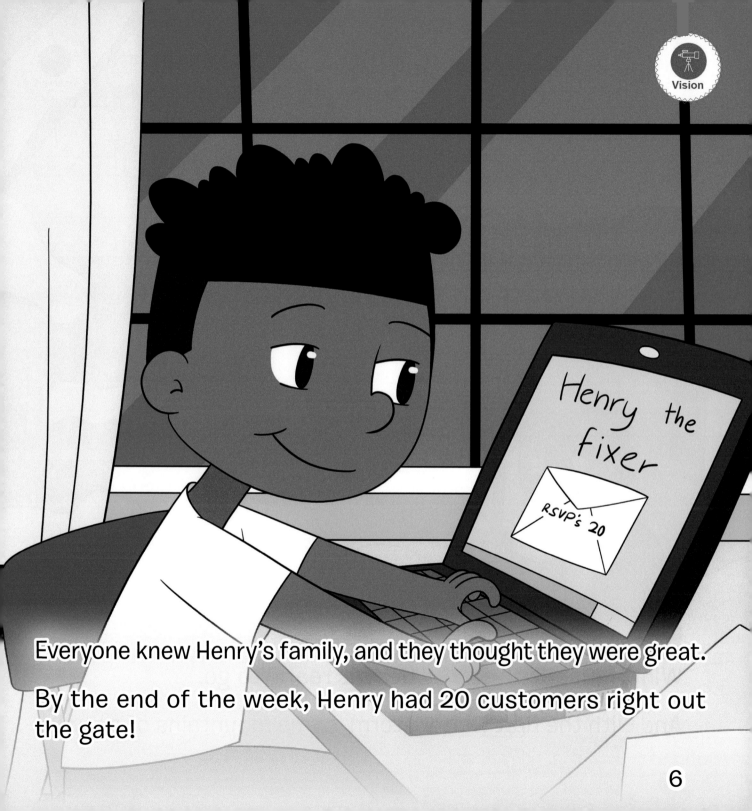

Everyone knew Henry's family, and they thought they were great.

By the end of the week, Henry had 20 customers right out the gate!

6

Winter just started and he was ready to go.

And with the first winter storm, came mountains of snow!

With his shovel in hand, he cleared sidewalks, driveways, and more.

And finished every job, despite being cold to his core!

Hardwork

8

Winter was gone, Spring brought flowers galore.

And Henry was back, going door to door!

He helped build ponds and planted many trees.

And thought to himself "I love this spring breeze!"

Next came Summer with a sun that was beaming.

The grass grew so tall, Henry thought he was dreaming!

With more daylight, Henry worked late through the evenings.

And would often remind himself "it's for a good reason!"

Finally, it was the Fall, Henry's favorite time of the year.

The weather was perfect and brought his heart a lot of cheer!

He loved seeing the colorful leaves that fell so frequent.

After bagging them away, every yard looked so decent!

The seasons were over, what a super fun race!

Now to count the money, in his hidden suitcase!

15

With his new stash of cash, he was closer than ever.

To planning a trip his family would treasure!

Christmas day came again, Henry's family together.

And at the right time, Henry gave out his letters!

And so Henry shouted – "Please, now open your gifts!"
We're going on a trip to see Aunt Vic!"

At that moment their faces said it all – Henry's hard work
and kindness all paid off!

The End!

Printed in the United States
by Baker & Taylor Publisher Services